The Mouse
and the Meadow

Written and Illustrated by Chad Wallace
Dawn Publications

Library of Congress Cataloging-in-Publication Data

Wallace, Chad.
The mouse and the meadow / by Chad Wallace. -- First edition.
pages cm
Summary: When a little mouse sets out to explore the meadow that is his home, he is taught and helped by many other creatures, from a spider spinning a web to a friendly band of fireflies lighting up the sky.
ISBN 978-1-58469-481-6 (hardback) -- ISBN 978-1-58469-482-3 (pbk.) [1. Stories in rhyme. 2. Mice--Fiction. 3. Meadow animals--Fiction. 4. Meadows--Fiction.] I. Title.
PZ8.3.W15845Mou 2014
[E]--dc23   2013027061

Book design and computer production by Patty Arnold, Menagerie Design and Publishing

Manufactured by Regent Publishing Services, Hong Kong
Printed January, 2014, in ShenZhen, Guangdong, China

10 9 8 7 6 5 4 3 2 1
First Edition

Dawn Publications
12402 Bitney Springs Road
Nevada City, CA 95959
530-274-7775
nature@dawnpub.com

One day a little meadow mouse was crawling through a field,
Staring in amazement at the wonders it revealed.
The grassy open meadow put his courage to the test,
For he had never left the comfort of his mother's nest.

He set out on his own to gain some knowledge of the earth,
To experience the lessons that would shape his sense of worth.
Among some tangled reeds he saw a spider weaving thread.
"What is it you're doing there?" the little rodent said.

"I'll trap myself some insects with this sticky silver lace.
There'll be no escaping once the webbing is in place."
The young mouse watched intently until finally she was done.
He marveled at the neat design the crafty spider spun.

And as he continued on among the flowers, leaves, and weeds,
The mouse soon found another creature tending to its needs.
A black and yellow honeybee was busy at her task.
"Excuse me!" said the mouse. "There is a question I must ask.
I see that you are busy, but would you please give mention
As to why that yellow flower is in need of your attention?"

"I'm out collecting pollen and sweet nectar for the hive;
Pollinating flowers so we all can stay alive."
He watched her gather nectar from the blossom's shiny crown.
She wore the golden pollen like a sticky yellow gown.
"I really must be going," the busy bee began to plead,
"I do have over thirty thousand mouths I need to feed."

With every new discovery his fascination grew
For the wonders of the meadow (from a mouse's point of view).
He scurried up a milkweed plant to find a higher seat,
And there he found a caterpillar hanging from its feet!
"Wow!" said the excited mouse, "That really looks like fun!"
Completely unaware a transformation had begun.

"Thirteen days," the larva spoke, "inside a chrysalis,
Where I will undergo a total metamorphosis!"

The humble rodent left the brilliant insect to her chore,
But he would need a break before proceeding to explore.
And so the tired mouse had come to rest upon a stone,
When suddenly he realized he no longer was alone!

The shiny boulder sprang to life and out emerged a head!
It would seem the unsuspecting mouse had been misled.
"Excuse me!" said the startled mouse, "I thought you were a mound!
You fooled me into thinking you were made of solid ground!"

"Don't give it a second thought," the old box turtle spoke,
"I like keeping company with harmless younger folk.
You see . . . not every creature in this meadow is your friend.
Some will introduce you to a most untimely end."

The mouse gave his attention to the turtle's candid words,
Which warned the mouse of hidden snakes and predatory birds.
So far he was fond of all the dwellers in this 'hood,
That is until he came upon a patch of rotting wood . . .

Something in the darkness raised the hair up on his back!
The frightened rodent feared he was the victim of attack!
Remembering the wise old turtle's warning to beware,
He ducked behind some thorns without a moment left to spare!

Lunging from the shadows was a giant hungry snake!
"You just made a most delectable missss-take!
You wandered in my territory. Now this is the deal:
You will have the honor of becoming my next meal!"

The serpent plunged his head inside the twisted, tangled shrub,
And slipped about the pricker bush in chase of yummy grub.
Then suddenly the reptile, whose cover had been blown,
Found that garter snakes are not the masters of this zone . . .

A weasel had the munchies for a long and scaly treat.
(Who would have thought that snakes are something weasels like to eat?)
So while the giant monsters kept each other held at bay,
It gave the frightened mouse the perfect chance to get away.

He came upon a grassy hole, but found it occupied—
A mother rabbit caring for the babies at her side.
He counted seven bunnies, snuggled tight upon her chest,
Safe and soundly sleeping in their warm and cozy nest.
"Hello!" said the gentle mom. "What brings you to my den?"

"It's dangerous outside," he said, "I won't go there again!"

"There's danger," said the rabbit, "in this meadow where we live,
But also it's a place to learn what nature has to give.
Every creature in this field, and in the sky above,
Plays a part in making this the meadow that we love.
Each day helps prepare us for the bumpy road ahead."
And then the sleepy mouse enjoyed a warm and fluffy bed.

"The mother rabbit's lesson was encouraging and wise,"
Thought the waking rodent as he rubbed open his eyes.
The little guy was not aware of all the hours passed,
But knew the sun was setting by the shadows that were cast.

"Thank you," said the tiny mouse. "I'd best be on my way.
I need to make my own home in the meadow right away!"
So once again he ventured out into the world unknown,
Wondering if one day he'll have bunnies of his own.

Next the mouse was witness to a most amazing sight:
Tiny insects dancing in a symphony of light!
A friendly band of fireflies was lighting up the sky,
Brilliant yellow flashes like the Fourth Day of July.
One of those glow bugs brightened up a nearby leaf.
"How is it you do that?" asked the mouse in disbelief.

"A chemical reaction makes our yellow bottoms glow.
It shows us where to find attractive females down below."

The conversation ended when from somewhere in the dark,
A stealthy bird of prey had made our meadow mouse its mark!
The fireflies were flickering, like torches on a path,
To help the fleeing mouse escape the predatory wrath!

He scrambled down a rocky trail; his body got the chills!
"That fast approaching owl is the kind of bird that kills!"
It swooped in right behind him like a wave upon a beach,
The great horned owl nearly had a mouse within its reach.

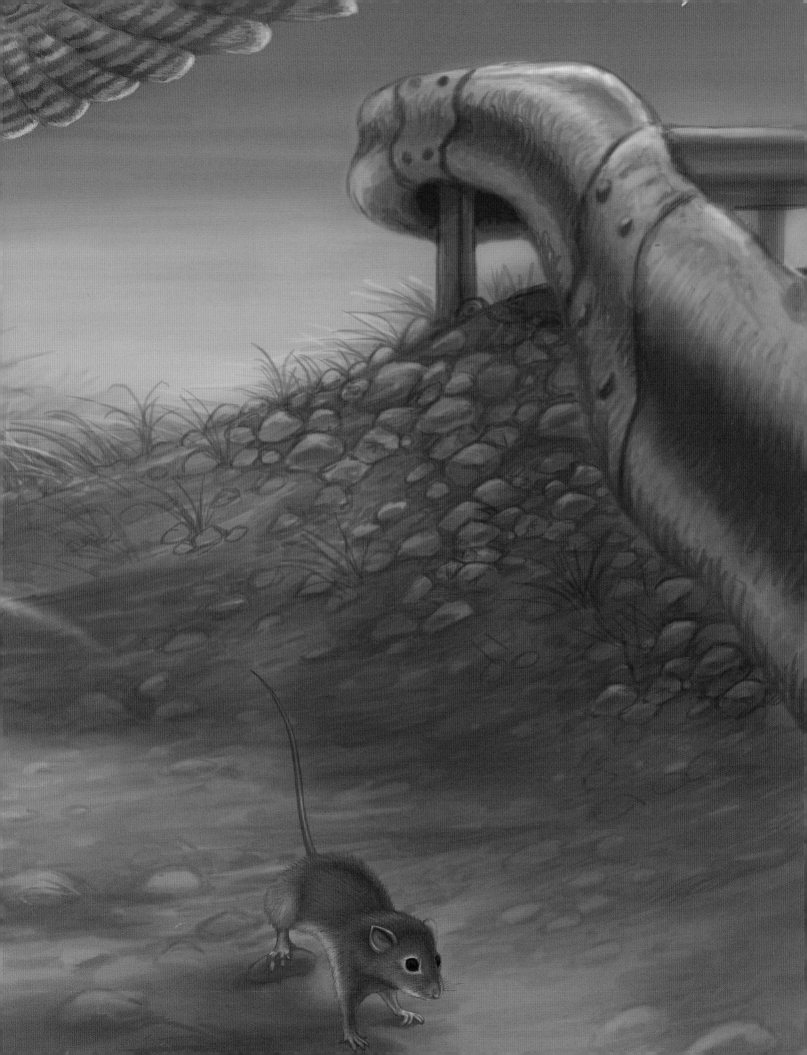

But just before the meadow mouse was taken in its grip,
An unexpected hero helped him give the bird the slip.
Another little mouse had come to save his skinny tail,
By pulling him to safety underneath a metal rail.

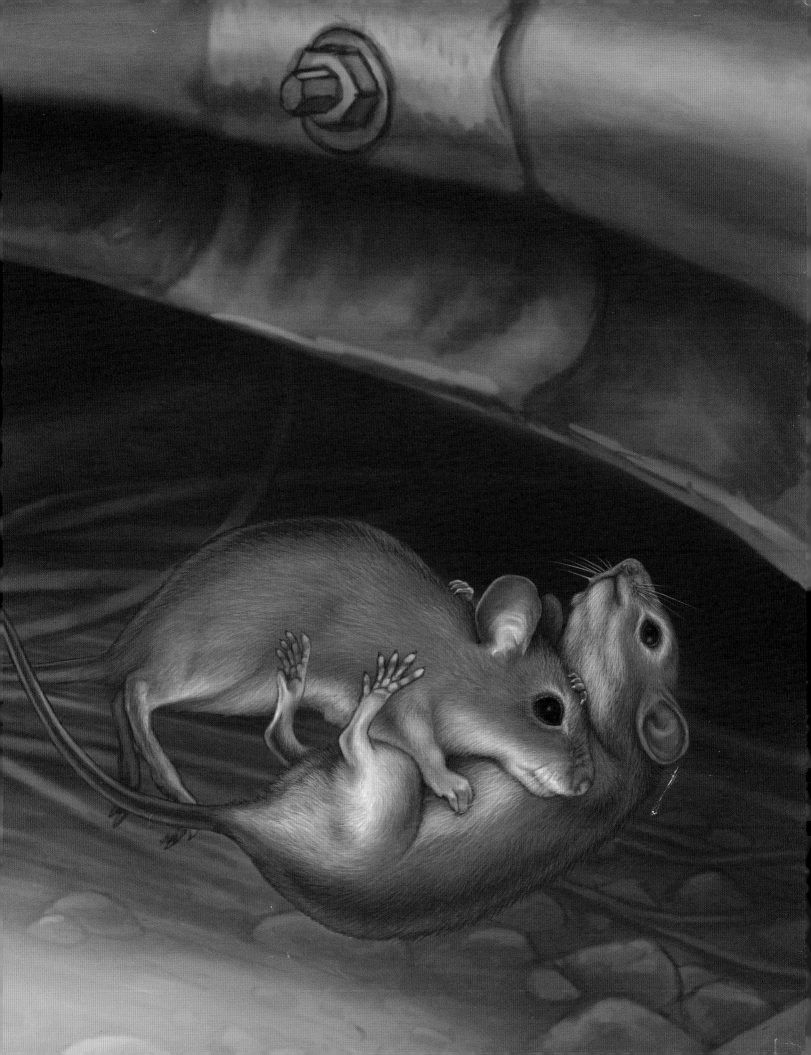

"Thank you!" said the shaken mouse, "I was almost food!
That bird came out of nowhere in a snacking kind of mood!"

She peered into his nervous eyes and volunteered a grin,
"You have no idea," she said, "the trouble WE get in!"

The whiskers on their faces glistened in the summer moon,
While a frog and cricket chorus sang a country meadow tune.
They sat there underneath the stars discussing nature's way,
To better be prepared to face the challenge of the day.

Animals that Talk?

Many stories about animals, including this one, intertwine fact with fiction. Animals do not "talk" like humans, but they do communicate, and we are beginning to understand how. Mice communicate using their mouths, noses, ears, and bodies. They make squeaks that are mostly outside the range of what humans can hear, although we can hear some of their lowest squeaks. Their meadow neighbors, the prairie dogs, have a very advanced language. See www.conslobodchikoff.com. The fireflies in this story were also signaling each other by making distinctive flashes of light. The honey bee in this story also "talks" to other bees by dancing in a very particular way that tells other bees precisely the direction and distance of flowers and the quality of their nectar or pollen. Some other species, such as whales and dolphins, have complex languages that people are beginning to understand. But can one species, such as the mouse in this story, communicate with animals of different species? Perhaps, but probably not nearly as well as in the story!

Animal Altruism

The little mouse in the story received help from other residents of the meadow—the box turtle warned of danger, the mother rabbit gave him a place to rest, and another mouse saved him from a deadly attack. Do you think a mother rabbit would give shelter to a young mouse? Do you think that one mouse might help save another mouse from an owl attack? Does cooperation really exist in the natural world? For many years scientists have studied animal cooperation and animal *altruism*—an act in which an animal sacrifices its own well-being for the benefit of another. One scientific explanation for animal cooperation is that animals help each other if they get something in return (*symbiosis* or *mutualism*). Another explanation is that animals help individuals within their same family group or species. Some scientists believe that animals are only altruistic when it promotes their survival.

Although we might not know the reasons animals help one another, many such behaviors have been observed.

- For days, a group of sperm whales swam and played with a handicapped bottlenose dolphin. Conversely, in New Zealand a bottlenose dolphin came to the rescue of two beached whales and led them into safe waters.
- In the wild, a leopard "adopted" a baby baboon.
- In captivity, a domestic cat has nursed baby bobcats and a dog has nursed lion cubs.
- Some Florida scrub jays take on the role of "parent helper," feeding chicks that aren't their own.
- Dolphins help sick or injured dolphins survive by pushing them up to the surface so they can breathe.
- "Cleaner fish," such as wrasses, nibble dead skin and parasites from large, predatory groupers without being eaten.
- Some meerkats act as sentinels and warn of approaching predators with an alarm call.
- A vampire bat regurgitates some of its meal (blood) to feed another bat that is hungry.
- Wolves and wild dogs carry food from a kill to share with other members of the pack.

Use these and other examples as a springboard for a discussion about animal behaviors. An excellent resource is *Do Animals Have Feelings, Too?* by David L. Rice (Dawn Publications, 1999). You can read more about the science related to animal altruism at goodnature.nathab.com/is-animal-altruism-real/.

Meadow Mice

A meadow mouse is also called a meadow vole or a field mouse. They are often the most common mammals in a meadow. They are active both day and night, especially when living under dense cover. Mice build a network of trails and tunnels in the grass as they travel throughout the meadow searching for food. Their diet includes grass, roots, seeds, grain, hay, vegetables, plant tubers, and the bark of trees. Meadow mice play an important role in the food web and are prey for many predators, including shrews, weasels, foxes, snakes, coyotes, hawks, and owls. Consequently the lifespan of a meadow mouse is often short, rarely more than a year in the wild.

However, meadow mice are extremely prolific, producing five to as many as ten litters a year with two to nine babies in a litter. Meadow mice live their lives right under our noses, often going completely unnoticed by humans. Look for these signs to find out if meadow mice are living near you:

- Small, raised tunnels near the surface.
- Black, oval droppings about the size of rice grains.
- Gnaw marks on trees or the wood of buildings.

Meadow Magic

A meadow is a community of grasses and wildflowers. It's sometimes called a prairie, grassland, or field. Meadows are an important environment. They act like sponges to absorb water and prevent run-off, and the root systems of meadow plants help hold the soil together and prevent erosion. Plants of different heights provide layers of shelter and cover for a wide variety of insects, reptiles, birds, and small mammals.

- There's lots of magic in a meadow! One example is the amazing *metamorphosis* (transformation) in the life cycle of a monarch from a tiny egg and caterpillar through the chrysalis stage to its emergence as an adult butterfly. Visit these web sites to learn more, see photos, and to participate in citizen science projects: www.monarchwatch.org and climatekids.nasa.gov/butterfly-garden/

- Find excellent information about animals, their habitats, and relationships at the Island Creek Elementary School ecology website, www.fcps.edu/islandcreekes/ecology.htm

Meadow Match-Up

The meadow is a complex ecosystem of relationships between plants and animals. In the following game, children review the relationships introduced in the story as they find their "meadow match."

1. Before playing, help children identify the matches mentioned in the story. Some relationships are between predator and prey. Notice that the mouse has two different possible matches: spider—insect (predator—prey); bee— flower blossom; milkweed plant—caterpillar; weasel—snake (predator—prey); owl—mouse (predator—prey); snake—mouse (predator—prey).

2. Using a clothespin, attach a photo/drawing of one of the animals to the front of each child's shirt. At your signal, have children find their match. Once everyone has found the correct match, have these partners act out a scene from the story in which they are the main characters. Students may pantomime the scene as you re-read the section of the story, or create their own dialog. For greater variety add additional meadow plant and animal pairs, such as: grasshopper—grass; deer—grass; frog—grasshopper (predator—prey); butterfly—wildflower; hawk—rabbit (predator—prey); ants—dead coyote; meadowlark—spider (the spider is prey to the meadowlark and a predator to an insect).

Miniature Meadow

Grow a miniature meadow in your schoolyard or garden. Most of the wildflowers found in "a meadow in a can" are suitable for a range of climate zones. Typically they're annuals, which grow rapidly the first year, providing an abundance of color quickly. Perennial mixes take longer to become established. Wildflower mixes specific to your area are often available at local garden supply stores and through your state's Native Plant Society. Have children keep a journal as they observe the flowers germinate, grow, and blossom.

- Find tips for growing a wildflower garden and curriculum ideas in "Native Beauty: Planting Wildflowers" at www.kidsgardening.org/node/12046.

- Order seeds and get planting suggestions at www.prairienursery.com or www.stockseed.com

The Name Means the Same

Introduce children to the concept that the same plant or animal may be called by different names—*synonyms*. Beginning with examples from this book, create a "Name Means the Same" bulletin board to collect synonyms.

meadow = field, grassland, or prairie

meadow vole = field mouse or meadow mouse

snake = serpent or reptile

firefly = glow bug or lightning bug

CHAD WALLACE grew up hiking and camping in Bear Mountain, New York, just west of the Hudson River. He loves the outdoors and frequently creates art inspired by natural settings. His art invites the viewer to experience emotions from the point of view of his subjects. Chad earned a BFA degree from Syracuse University and a master's degree at the Fashion Institute of Technology. He has illustrated nine books, but *The Mouse and the Meadow* is his first authored work. Two of his earlier books for Dawn Publications — *Pass the Energy, Please!* and *Earth Day Birthday* — were crafted with traditional media. In this book he accomplishes a full transition to electronic art by simultaneously preparing the book for print, ebook, and app/game editions. The often unnoticed, under-appreciated beauty of meadow life has not escaped the attention of this award-winning author/illustrator.

New From Dawn ∽ Interactive Book Apps

The Mouse and the Meadow—Experience the vibrant nature of meadow life by helping Mouse navigate his way, making new friends, avoiding danger, all at the tips of little fingers!

The Swamp Where Gator Hides—Look for gator hiding in the algae, then animate the turtle, vole, bobcat, duck, sunfish, and other animals that might be his lunch.

Noisy Frog Sing-Along—Touch the noisy frogs and watch their bulgy throat pouches expand. Then play the game, matching their sounds (and sound waves) with each kind of frog.

Noisy Bug Sing-Along—Listen to a chorus of insect sounds and watch how they make those sounds by moving different body parts! Then play the matching game.

Over in the Ocean—Little fingers can make the octopus squirt, and the pufferfish puff! Then take the counting game challenge to find all 55 babies hiding in the coral reef.

Over in the Jungle—As you touch each baby, watch the ocelots pounce, parrots squawk, and boas squeeze – and then find all the babies hiding in the jungle floor and canopy.

Some Other Animal Stories From Dawn Publications

Eliza and the Dragonfly—almost despite herself, Eliza becomes entranced by the "awful" dragonfly nymph—and before long, both of them are transformed.

Forest Bright, Forest Night—Peek into a forest by daytime to see who is awake and who is asleep. Then flip the book to see the same—yet very different!—scenes at night.

Gobble, Gobble—Arrow-shaped footprints lead Jenny through a year of enchantment as she shares her discovery of these wonderful birds. Gobble, gobble!

Granny's Clan—Life as a wild orca (killer) whale is very much a family affair. Here is the true story of Granny, a 100 year-old whale matriarch, and how she teaches young whales and helps her magnificent clan to survive.

In the Trees, Honey Bees offers an inside-the-hive view of a wild colony, along with solid information about these remarkable and valuable creatures.

On Kiki's Reef—From egg to gentle giant, a green sea turtle's life introduces the magical, hidden world of sea turtles.

Dawn Publications is dedicated to inspiring in children a deeper understanding and appreciation for all life on Earth. You can browse through our titles, download resources for teachers, and order at www.dawnpub.com or call 800-545-7475.